*For Jennifer, my beautiful, brilliant wife. Forever my inspiration
and the true Queen of the Dinosaurs. —DK*

*For Ansley, who has grown, and for Anthony, who will.
And for Paul, who makes all things possible. —AQ*

ABOUT THIS BOOK

The illustrations for this book were done with Gansai Tambi watercolors and Tombow ink pens on Fabariano Artistico hot-press watercolor paper. This book was edited by Mary-Kate Gaudet and designed by Véronique Lefèvre Sweet. The production was supervised by Bernadette Flinn, and the production editor was Marisa Finkelstein. The text was set in Nicolas Cochin Regular, and the display type is the artist's hand lettering.

Text copyright © 2021 by Daniel Kibblesmith • Illustrations copyright © 2021 by Ashley Quach. Cover illustration copyright © 2021 by Ashley Quach. Cover design by Véronique Lefèvre Sweet. • Cover copyright © 2021 by Hachette Book Group, Inc. • Hachette Book Group supports the right to free expression and the value of copyright. The purpose of copyright is to encourage writers and artists to produce the creative works that enrich our culture. • The scanning, uploading, and distribution of this book without permission is a theft of the author's intellectual property. If you would like permission to use material from the book (other than for review purposes), please contact permissions@hbgusa.com. Thank you for your support of the author's rights. • Little, Brown and Company • Hachette Book Group • 1290 Avenue of the Americas, New York, NY 10104 • Visit us at LBYR.com • First Edition: January 2021 • Little, Brown and Company is a division of Hachette Book Group, Inc. • The Little, Brown name and logo are trademarks of Hachette Book Group, Inc. • The publisher is not responsible for websites (or their content) that are not owned by the publisher. • Library of Congress Cataloging-in-Publication Data • Names: Kibblesmith, Daniel, 1983– author. | Quach, A.P. (Ashley Perryman), illustrator. • Title: Princess Dinosaur / written by Daniel Kibblesmith ; illustrated by Ashley Quach. • Description: First edition. | New York : Little, Brown and Company, 2021. | Audience: Ages 4-8. | Summary: "A spirited and expectation-defying story of a heroine who embraces two seemingly opposed aspects of her personality; she's a princess and a dinosaur!"—Provided by publisher. • Identifiers: LCCN 2019031301 | ISBN 9780316457606 (hardcover) • Subjects: CYAC: Stories in rhyme. | Dinosaurs—Fiction. | Princesses—Fiction. • Classification: LCC PZ8.3.K52 Pri 2021 | DDC [E]—dc23 • LC record available at https://lccn.loc.gov/2019031301 • ISBN: 978-0-316-45760-6 (hardcover) • PRINTED IN CHINA • APS • 10 9 8 7 6 5 4 3 2 1

Princess Dinosaur

Written by **Daniel Kibblesmith**

Illustrated by **Ashley Quach**

Ⓛ Ⓑ

Little, Brown and Company · New York Boston

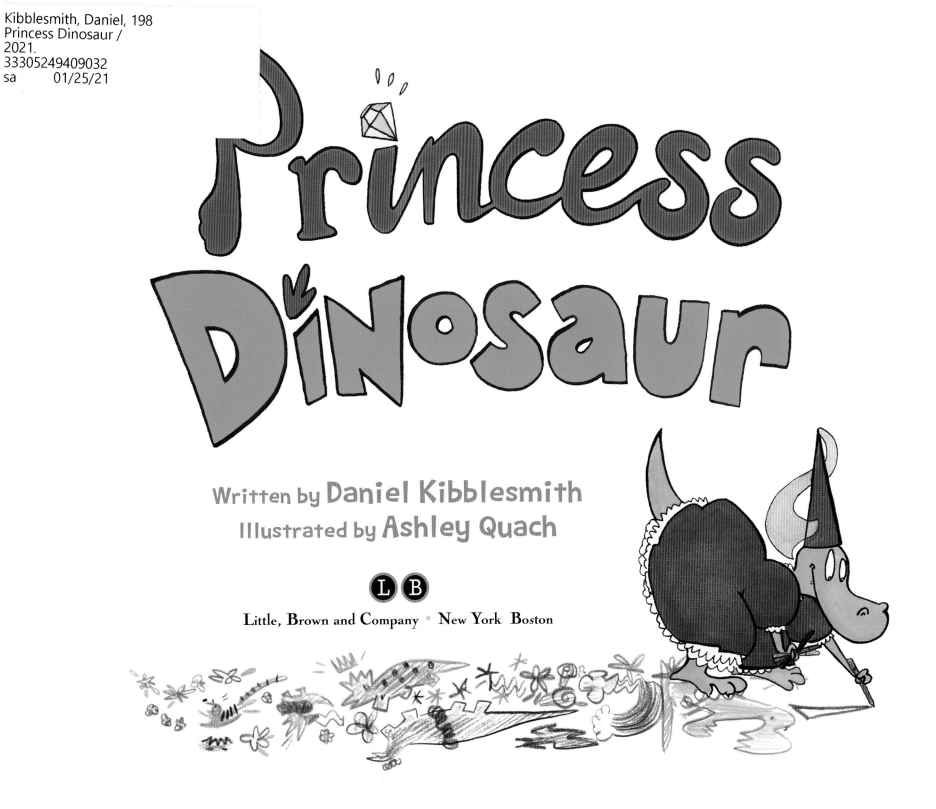

This is Princess Dinosaur.

Listen to the princess!

She's ferocious as can be.

She also hosts a lovely tea.

Princess Dinosaur stalks her prey.

Princess Dinosaur does ballet.

First she screams and stomps her feet!

Then she can be *oh so sweet.*

Her table manners can be crude.

She's picky about certain food.

Her dino claws
are razor sharp.

She uses them
to play her harp.

The princess sometimes
breaks the rules...

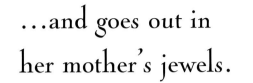...and goes out in
her mother's jewels.

Or colors on the palace walls.
Or gives a haircut to her dolls.

Or lets out her INNER BEAST!

And gets time-out…
'til she's released.

Her favorite color
is always pink.

Except when it's red, or blue, or
yellow, or green, or orange, or
purple, or silver, or rainbow,
or clear, or light periwinkle
with chartreuse polka dots.

Dinosaurs are wild and free.

With no responsibility.

Princesses are kind and warm.
And keep their subjects safe from harm.

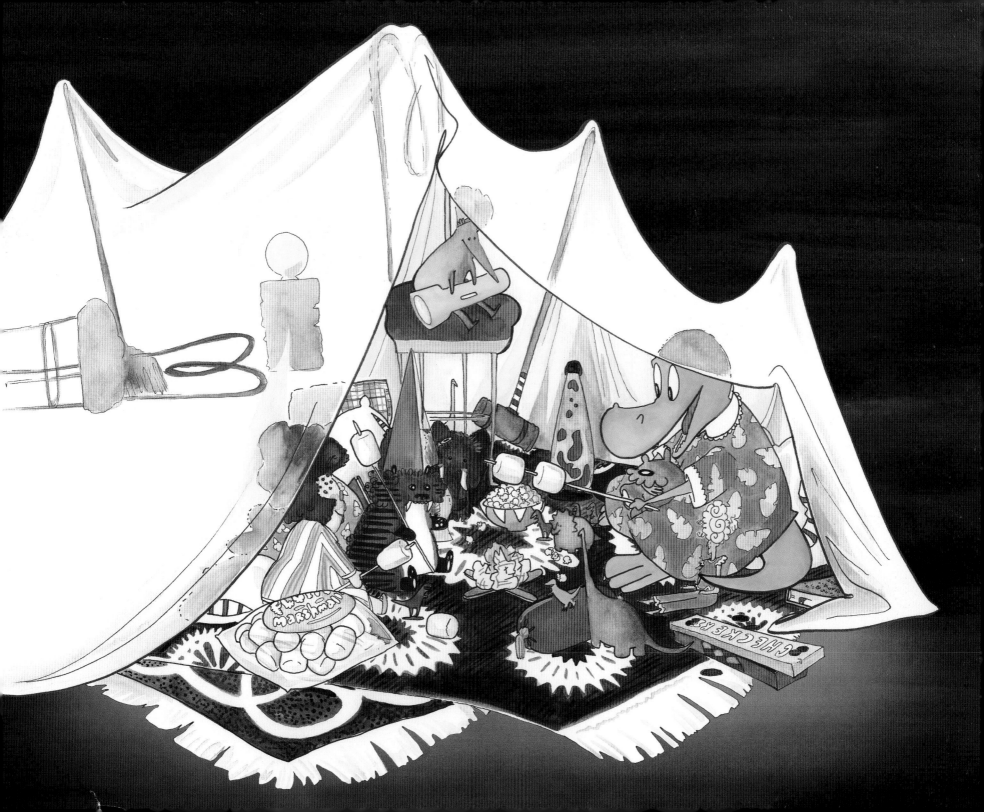

A princess can BE a dinosaur.
But they can also be much, much more!

Like AN ASTRONAUT- SOCCER PLAYER- COWBOY- SCUBA DIVER.

MOVIE STAR-
VETERINARIAN-
PRESIDENT
OF THE UNITED STATES!

So if you stomp
your feet and

and wear *Fancy* dresses from the store,

you might be one thing,
or two, or more.

Like a princess
AND a dinosaur.